August Kluckhohn, Elisabeth Harriet Denio

Louise, Queen of Prussia

A memorial

August Kluckhohn, Elisabeth Harriet Denio

Louise, Queen of Prussia
A memorial

ISBN/EAN: 9783337298838

Printed in Europe, USA, Canada, Australia, Japan

Cover: Foto ©Raphael Reischuk / pixelio.de

More available books at **www.hansebooks.com**

LOUISE,

QUEEN OF PRUSSIA.

A Memorial.

BY

AUGUST KLUCKHOHN.

TRANSLATED FROM THE GERMAN

BY

ELIZABETH H. DENIO,

TEACHER OF GERMAN IN WELLESLEY COLLEGE.

CAMBRIDGE:

Printed at the Riverside Press.

1881.

To

DR. C. A. F. MAHN,

PROFESSOR IN THE ACADEMY OF MODERN LANGUAGES AT BERLIN, GERMANY,

This Little Work

IS AFFECTIONATELY INSCRIBED

BY

THE TRANSLATOR.

LOUISE, QUEEN OF PRUSSIA.

THE day on which, one hundred years ago, Louise, afterwards Queen of Prussia, beheld the light of this world, deserves to be honored by all Germans as one of the great memorial days in their country's history. The life and sufferings of the noble Princess are joined most closely with a significant and distinct part of Germany's past, and the blessed consequences of her deeds endure even to the present.

The mother of the illustrious Emperor William early awakened and nourished in him those high virtues which we hope may long prove an ornament to the German imperial throne, and conduce to the welfare of the people. This noble woman, in the days of the deepest abasement of Germany, in spite of unutterable sorrow, was full of confidence in God and full of faith in the better future of the Fatherland. She inspired souls and strengthened hearts. At last, when the hour of deliverance struck, and the whole nation, in enthusiastic devotion to the great cause, went forth

to an earnest and victorious contest, the memory
of her and others, in glory, served to fill the cham-
pions of the Fatherland with an ideal sentiment,
and to bequeath to their sons and grandsons an
inexhaustible treasure of moral power.   Were not
all, too, who were witnesses of the events of 1870
and 1871, often reminded of the struggles for
liberty in 1813 and 1814, and of Queen Louise?
In fact, she belongs not to Prussia alone, but to
the entire German nation.   Queen Louise was de-
scended, on her father's side, from the princely
house of Mecklenburg; on her mother's side, from
the house of Hesse-Darmstadt.   Her father, Louis
Frederick von Mecklenburg - Strelitz, was then
Field-Marshal in the service of Hanover.   Louise
was born in Hanover, March 10, 1776.   Her
mother was the Princess Frederika Caroline Louise von Hesse-Darmstadt, who, March 22, 1782,
was taken by death from her husband and ten
children, among whom Louise was the sixth.
Louise, with her three sisters, was intrusted to the
care of a Fräulein von Wolzogen, to whom superior mental gifts are attributed.   She found com-
pensation for the mother lost so early, in her father's second wife, her mother's sister.   When
this wife died, the Duke returned in sorrow to
Darmstadt to give the half-orphaned children into
the care of their grandmother, the Landgravine
Maria Louise Albertina.

A Swiss lady, Fräulein von Gelieux, was appointed governess to the Princess, and as she had been educated in French, she gave the lessons in French instead of in the German language. Thus Louise learned in her youth to speak and write French with perfect facility, according to the prevailing custom in aristocratic circles at that time, while German remained neglected. This deficiency she deplored, and sought later to supply, even when Queen, by industrious study of German writers.

Although the education of the Princess in her youth was almost entirely conducted in French, yet it had nothing in it of foreign superficiality. Louise often said in praise of her governess, for whom to the end of her life she preserved a touching attachment and gratitude, that she early directed her attention to higher things, and brought her to a knowledge of God in this life. With genuine and simple piety, and deep sympathy for the sorrows of others, Louise, even as a child, combined an active impulse to help. Clinging to the hand of her governess, one could see the little Princess often searching out the cottages of poverty, in order to aid the needy and suffering as far as her small means allowed. The seriousness of her temperament was profoundly moved by the heavy strokes of fate which had come upon her

father's house. As must be the case in every
healthful and gifted nature, trouble did not ex-
clude a childlike, cheerful disposition, and suscep-
tibility to the pleasures of a rural life.

A new world opened before the eyes of the
youthful Louise when, under the oversight of her
grandmother, she made her first journey of any
length.

She visited an aunt, the wife of Duke Maximil-
ian von Zweibrücken (afterwards the first King
of Bavaria), in Strasburg, in order to travel from
Alsace down the Rhine to the Netherlands. It
was a pleasant sight to watch the Princess climb
the gigantic pile of the Minster, from the plat-
form of which she looked with rapture out into
the glorious border-land which, torn from Germany by French trickery, her son and grandson,
at the head of the united German armies, were
to win back to the new Empire. No less did the
populous cities of the Netherlands and the magnificent beauty of the ocean make a vivid impression upon her.

Quite often visits were made from Darmstadt to
neighboring Frankfort. Louise looked upon the
solemn spectacle of the coronation of the last two
German Emperors, who were crowned in Frankfort in 1790 and 1791. She passed, with her brothers and sisters, happy hours in Goethe's father's
house, hours which were never forgotten by the

mother of the " Prince of poets," nor by Louise.
What " Frau Rath " told of this visit to Bettina
(Elizabeth von Arnim), caused the latter to sketch
that life-like picture of the stay of Louise which
is found in " Goethe's Correspondence with a
Child," under the date of March 5, 1808. The
Princess, together with her grandmother, remained
longer at Hildburghausen, where her elder sister
Charlotte was married to the reigning Duke. The
beautiful days which Louise passed in charming
Thüringia were never forgotten by her. Even
better remembered was the return-trip in the
spring of 1793, when the Landgravine, with Louise and her younger sister, took the route, by way
of Frankfort, in order that the old lady might pay
respects to her nephew, King Frederick William
II., of Prussia. From the appearance of the first
war of the German powers against revolutionary
France, he had his headquarters in Frankfort.
The grandmother presented her granddaughters
to the King, and when she planned to resume her
journey the same evening she was induced to
defer her departure by an invitation to take sup-
per with the King and the two Princes accompa-
nying him.

It was on this evening that Louise, then seventeen years of age, radiant with magical grace and
noble beauty, made such a charming impression

upon the Crown Prince Frederick William that
the first glance decided his choice. The deep
affection of the Prince, whose stately appearance
was still more enhanced by the simple nobility
of his nature, was returned by Louise. At the
same time, the younger brother, Prince Louis, felt
himself drawn towards Frederika, the beautiful
sister of Louise. After a month, April 24, 1793,
the festival of a double betrothal was celebrated
at Darmstadt.

During the campaign that followed soon after,
on the left bank of the Rhine, the two Princesses
visited with their grandmother their betrothed,
and ventured several times into the varied life of
the camp. The youthful Goethe, then at the
Prussian headquarters, gives an account of one of
these visits, in the following manner: " Toward
evening there was prepared for us, but especially
for me, a lovely sight. The Princesses of Mecklenburg had dined at the headquarters of His
Majesty the King, and after dinner visited the
camp. I confined myself to my tent, and could
thus most perfectly observe the high-born person-
ages, who walked up and down before me quite at
their ease. In this tumult of war, one might
really consider the two Princesses as heavenly vis-
ions. The impression which they made upon me
will never be obliterated."

Toward the end of the year the Crown Prince returned to Berlin. His fiancée, with the sister betrothed to Prince Louis, soon followed him to Berlin, where a grand reception was prepared for her by the citizens. Festive was the entrance into the city, sincere and great the universal joy. The majestic beauty and remarkable grace of the Crown Princess, the enchanting affability and goodness which beamed from her youthful countenance, won to her all hearts. Fouqué remarks : " The arrival of the angelic Princess spreads over these days a noble splendor. All hearts go out to meet her, and her grace and goodness leaves no one unblessed." The venerable Mistress of the Robes, Oberhofmeisterin von Voss, recently assigned to the Princess, did not find her childlike, frank, impulsive demeanor sufficiently ceremonious. When Louise, entering Berlin, was greeted under a triumphal arch by eighty children clothed in white, with garlands of flowers and a festive poem, she lifted up to her the little speaker, to the delight of the thronging people, and, overpowered by emotion, clasped the child in her arms and kissed her. The Oberhofmeisterin, sitting opposite the Princess in the great golden chariot of state, said, alarmed : " Mein Gott, what has Your Royal Highness done ; that is against all etiquette ! " " How, may I not do that any longer?" was, according to report, the exact answer. A week later, this strict guardian of etiquette wrote in her diary: " The Princess is really adorable, so good, and at the same time so charming, an angel." In the notes of the following year it is said: " The more perfectly one becomes acquainted with the Princess the more is one captivated by the inner nobility, and the angelic goodness of her heart."

The marriage ceremony took place on the evening before Christmas in the " White Hall " of the royal palace, and festival followed festival. But to the newly wedded pair did their quiet domestic life, far from the bustle of the court, afford greater satisfaction. The Crown Prince and Louise lived a genuine German family life, full of love and devotion, in glaring contrast to the French gallantry, not to say immorality, which then ruled in the higher circles of society. Externally, to be sure, the aristocratic world of the Prussian capital offered a dazzling picture. Those were the days when knightly men and witty women reveled in æsthetic enjoyments.

Sensual and intellectual pleasures were too often associated, and thus the strict discipline of earlier days was displaced by a refined irregularity of life. It is known that the court of Frederick William II. did not preserve its old-timed reputation for strictness of morals, but showed too much leniency to gallant adventurers. In contrast with this, the simple, pure family life of the Crown Prince and Louise furnished a shining example of the ancient virtuous training. This was due not alone to the pure and pious heart of the Princess, but also to the serious and deeply religious mind of the Crown Prince. Although but twenty-seven years old, he offered a firm support to his young wife, and by his devotion and truth knew how to keep far from her every distressing influence. Frederick William was in a high degree worthy of the possession of the noblest of women, and deserved the rare happiness which she brought to him. Louise gratefully acknowledged that she herself had become better through the husband, whom she entirely loved and honored as the "best of men."

Frederick William, in the society of his wife, maintained his right to the use of "Du," then unusual at courts. The unfeigned serenity and sincerity of home-life he would not allow to be disturbed by any ceremonies or ostentation. "I am already cramped and annoyed enough without this; I will, at least in my home, follow my inclination and have the freedom and independence that every private citizen enjoys."

The royal pair felt most happy in rural retire-
ment. Since life was not quiet and simple enough
at Oranienburg, which King Frederick William II.
had given to the daughter-in-law he so highly
honored, the Crown Prince fitted up the Paretz
estate on the Havel as a royal residence for the
summer. Here, with sunny Louise, he enjoyed
the simple pleasures of a country life, calling himself, in jest, the "Mayor of Paretz," while the
Crown Princess was pleased with "My Lady."
In harvest feasts she took part in the dances of
the peasants. Often, too, was this noble lady
seen at the village festivals, surrounded by the
youth, or, going from stall to stall, she purchased
small presents and distributed them among the
children, who would call out confidingly, "Some-
thing for me, too, Lady Queen!"

Louise permitted no opportunity to pass of add-
ing to the joys of others and of showing kindness
to the poor. King Frederick William II., who
extolled her as the "Princess among princesses,"
asked, on her first birthday-fête in Berlin, after
delighting her with rich gifts, if she had still a
wish. The Crown Princess wished for herself a
handful of money in order to let the poor people
of the capital share in her joy. With a smile the
King asked how great did she suppose a handful

of money to be. The answer runs : " As great as the heart of the most gracious of Kings." With royal liberality was her wish fulfilled.

It was the thought of being able to dispense benefactions to a greater degree that possessed the soul of Louise when her husband, after his father's death, ascended the Prussian throne, November 6, 1797. " I am now Queen," she wrote to her grandmother, " and what rejoices me most is the hope that now I need no longer count my benefactions so carefully."

Louise stood at the summit of prosperity, beloved and honored by all circles of the people, as rarely a queen has been. While one blessed her name on account of the benevolence which she practiced in secret, others praised the graciousness and kind condescension that she showed to every one, and again others honored her as an exalted pattern of all virtues. Artists and poets ceased not to glorify her as the sweetest and fairest of women. According to the testimony of contemporaries, no painter succeeded in doing her complete justice, because no one was able to reproduce " her winning glance so full of soul and goodness, especially in conversation." The old, distinguished secretary and soldier, Scheffner, declared : " I have never seen in any woman's face eyes of a purer, freer expression, such gladsome

ingenuousness, almost bordering upon childlike-
ness." We must listen to the voices of her contemporaries to have an idea of the magic that her
appearance produced.

" The Queen," writes an English lady, who
saw her at the close of the year 1800, " reminds
me of Burke's star, that irradiates life, light, and
joy.[1] She verified such extravagant representations as one gets in childhood from the ' Arabian
Nights ' of a young, beautiful, and glorious queen.
She is an angel in loveliness, gentleness, and
grace. Tall and slender, she is not deficient in a
suitable contour of form ; she has light hair, her
complexion is delicate and pure, the expression of
her face of indescribable graciousness." " She
had," as the Oberhofmeisterin expressed herself,
" an exceedingly beautiful figure, both noble and
lovely ; every one who saw her felt irresistibly
drawn to and attached to her." " Why can I
not," exclaims another lady of her time, after the
Queen's early decease, — " why can I not hold
fast such features of her noble image as still float

---

[1] " It is now sixteen or seventeen years since I saw the Queen
of France, then the Dauphiness, at Versailles ; and surely never
lighted on this orb, which she hardly seemed to touch, a more de-
lightful vision. I saw her just above the horizon, decorating and
cheering the elevated sphere she just began to move in ; glittering like the morning star, full of life, and splendor, and joy." —
Wisdom and Genius of Burke, p. 148.

fresh in my mind. The nameless grace of her greeting, the inimitable rhythm of her walk and bow, or the childlike repose of her gentle and yet earnest glance, or the gliding of her royal form into a splendid assembly in which, however large it might be, she appeared always the fairest, the first, the only one. Of her was true in its full sense Ossian's praise, 'Beautiful among thousands.' If one tried to compare others with her, and considered their forms more beautiful in single features, none stood the comparison. The character of her beauty lay in the harmony of her nature. Here prevailed tenderness, gentleness, and perfect naturalness."

With justice it has been noticed of Louise's sweet kindness, that she became a gentle bond of union between monarch and people ; where it was important to thank, to answer, to represent, she served the taciturn King as a mouthpiece. She accompanied her husband on the journey of homage to Königsberg, Warschau, and Breslau, also on many journeys later through the land. She found opportunity to show herself to the inhabitants of remote provinces, as a joy-dispensing mother of her country, who did not appear less winning in the peasant's cottage than in the splendor of the court.

Gladly did Frederick William and Louise, after

the accession to the throne, withdraw to Potsdam, Charlottenburg, and Paretz, and continued even in Berlin, the simple life of an earlier date. Along with her husband's love mother-love blessed the Queen. Frederick William, who afterwards was the fourth King of this name, was born in 1795, and William, the Emperor of the new Empire, in 1797. In the course of years were added two children, who died early, the two Princes, Carl and Albert, and the Princesses Charlotte, Alexandrina, and Louise. The two youngest, Albert and Louise, were born in Königsberg in the time of her calamity.

" To train my children to become benevolent lovers of mankind," she expresses herself in a letter of the year 1797, "is my warmest and dearest wish. I even nourish the glad hope of fulfilling my aim."

The leisure remaining to the Queen, after the exemplary fulfillment of her duties, she employed in nourishing her richly gifted mind with everything good and beautiful that literature offered her. By choice she devoted herself to the study of German poetry, which then began to send out its fairest blossoms. Herder, Goethe, Schiller, Jean Paul engaged her much. The latter dedicated " Titan " " to the four beautiful and noble sisters on the throne," and wrote a poem on the early death of Queen Louise called "Autumn Flowers." He wrote from Weimar, in November, 1800, that the Queen took even on the shortest journey one of Herder's works. In later years, as we are informed, she admired Goethe as the perfect master.

Thoughts of freedom and patriotic enthusiasm drew her to Schiller, who, in his last great creations, so gloriously gave expression to these sentiments. She would gladly have seen the poet of "The Maid of Orleans" ("Die Jungfrau von Orleans") and "Wilhelm Tell" remain in Berlin. Through translations she became acquainted with the Greek tragedians and the great English dramatist, and was also familiar with the most important works of history. Of that which the Queen read she lost nothing. It served for the ennobling of her mind and the deepening of her character. Although in her own consciousness she was a believing Christian, yet, from some of her later letters, we seem to catch sounds in harmony with ancient views of life.

Her manner of viewing the world rested on deep religious foundations. In the sunny days of prosperity, when shallow minds are wont to grow effeminate, she was strong; and heroic and submissive in bearing the hard strokes of fate which soon fell on her people and her own family.

2

Frederick William III., who came to the throne of the Hohenzollern line when twenty-seven, was a man of superior parts. He had an earnest, straight-forward, upright mind; in him dwelt simplicity, moderation, love of exact order, and strict principle. With the best motives he did not lack clearness and strength of mind; yet perhaps he was wanting in self-confidence and resolution for a sudden responsible action. He had not been well trained, and was accustomed to the society of mediocre and weak, although worthy, men. A certain timidity in the presence of great natures seemed characteristic. " Those that educated, surrounded, and served him," said the best critic of the Berlin court, " were all weak, and crippled, hindered, and disheartened him."

When Frederick William III., took the reins of government after his father's death, the state needed more than ever a judicious and firm guidance, in accordance with established principles. It was not sufficient that the new monarch esteemed highly economy and order in the administration of the government, that he put a speedy end to the scandal that was connected with Lichtenau and her followers, and, instead of the hypocrisy which Wöllner had favored by his " Edict of Religion," cared for and cultivated convincing godliness. It was a matter of great concern to

animate the life of the entire state, threatened
with rottenness, with a new spirit, by means of
thorough reforms, and, above all, to place foreign
affairs in able hands. But Frederick William,
fearing any extensive change, retained in the foreign service, and in his Cabinet, unprincipled and
cowardly men like Haugwitz and Lombard, who
urged the state of Frederick the Great along a
downward course. Without entering into partic-
ulars in regard to the much slandered policy of
Prussia at the end of the last and the beginning
of this century, it will be appropriate to bring
briefly to mind the following facts.

After the breaking out of the French Revolution, and its first threatening manifestations toward other countries, Prussia and Austria joined
hands in a common struggle. Influenced by the
Peace at Basel, Frederick William withdrew from
the war against France, not without the censure
of the suspicious and jealous Cabinet at Vienna.
Henceforth, while almost all Europe was filled
with contests, Prussia persisted in her feeble neutrality. Out of this she did not even come when
the issue was no longer the assistance of the German Empire, but when the honor and the position
of the state of Frederick the Great as a power was
in question.

In face of Napoleon's increased usurpations and

encroachments no one in Berlin could fail to believe that, instead of being intimidated by the French under a mask and show of friendship, it was of the utmost importance resolutely to draw the sword. We know how the King, already long pressed by a patriotic party, with which Louise sympathized, at last turned about completely and began to enter into closer relations with the powers allied against France.

The continual allurements and offers of alliance with Napoleon were refused. Meanwhile the people did not pluck up heart for participation in the war against Napoleon especially, because Austria and Russia did not take the right means to draw Prussia over to their side. Only the open violation of Prussian neutrality during the French and Austrian campaign of 1805 gave the war party in Berlin ascendency for the time being. Over the grave of Frederick II., Alexander of Russia and Frederick William III., joined hands in a league against Napoleon, to the keen joy of the Queen. Unfortunately when it was of moment to lay before Napoleon an ultimate decision, the King trusted the cowardly Haugwitz with the most important of missions. We know in what manner he discharged his office. Put off by the Emperor, even until the decisive battle of Austerlitz, the weak, dishonorable diplomatist converted the threat of war into a congratulation for the conqueror, and entered into negotiations with him concerning the importance of which, in the begining, he deceived his own monarch. The patriotic circle in Berlin was full of wrath on hearing of Haugwitz's disgraceful performances, and the King's sense of honor bristled up at being obliged to ratify a treaty with France, wrongfully required of him. Prussia, therefore, provoked Napoleon, and, on account of her isolated position, did not venture to engage in a contest with the arrogant Emperor, but concluded a treaty with him under even more unfavorable conditions. Meanwhile new humiliations and demands on the part of Napoleon, who now threw off his mask as regarded Prussia, followed quickly. The King at last decided on war against the Emperor of Battles, now, to be sure, at the wrong time, and under the most unfavorable circumstances.

Notwithstanding the warlike feeling in Berlin and the prestige of former victories, notwithstanding the remote prospect of help from Russia, the King, having his eyes opened, was not for a moment deceived in regard to Prussia's danger. Meanwhile Napoleon burned with desire to destroy at one blow the great state which he had cajoled when he fondly thought he could make it his tool, and subject the North of Germany as well as the South and Southwest to his dominion.

The imperfect conduct of the war and the condition of the army, spoiled by long peace, made victory only too easy for the mighty commander. A double battle, the day of misfortunes, at Jena and Auerstädt, decided the fate of the monarchy. Five weeks after the catastrophe of October 14, 1806, the conqueror entered Berlin.

As is well known, Napoleon had in his lying bulletins tried to make Queen Louise responsible for the war, and, with the vulgarity of which he was capable, slandered and laughed her to scorn. The Queen was staying at the Baths of Pyrmont, when the fateful war ended, and had no share at all in the momentous deliberations. A few days before the battle of Jena she remarked to Frederick Gentz, in a memorable audience, that she had never been consulted about public affairs, and did not aspire to be. On the same occasion the witty statesman and political writer was filled with admiration for the high bearing and noble sentiments, as well as the wisdom, delicacy, and independence of judgment " of the great, unhappy, and immortal Louise." With decision she repelled the idea of a preference for Russia, falsely attributed to her by the French, and did not conceal that, with all due recognition of the personal virtues of the Emperor Alexander, she never could consider Russia as a chief instrument for the deliverance of Europe, but she regarded assistance from her as the last source of aid. She was firmly convinced that " the great means of deliverance were only to be found in the closest union of all who felt proud of being of German stock."

Although the Queen had not advised war, after it was ended she no longer concealed that she approved of it, and showed herself brave and loyally devoted to her husband. She accompanied the King from Charlottenburg to Thüringia on the opening of the campaign. Here she remained near him until October 14th. Only when the thunder of battle rolled over toward Weimar did she, at her husband's command, hasten back by a circuitous route to the capital. The agitating news of the defeat of the army reached her at the gates of Berlin. She and her children sought protection in Stettin. When the disgraceful surrender of the best fortresses of the land and the sad fate of the dispersed armies completed the misfortune of Jena and Auerstädt she fled to Küstrin. Here she met her afflicted husband, but soon had to seek a refuge in Graudenz, and later in Königsberg, since the enemy, advancing rapidly, followed her everywhere. In those miserable days of treachery, when one terrible piece of news followed another, the Queen addressed words to the Princes, Frederick and William, which, better than I can express, make known the spirit of this sorrowful but heroic woman. " You see me in tears ; I lament the destruction of the army ! It has not answered to the expectations of the King." Thus she began, and continued, according to reports at that time, in the following manner : " Destiny has destroyed in one day a structure in the erection of which the great men of two centuries have labored. There is no Prussian state, no Prussian army, no national glory longer ; it has disappeared like that mist which on the fields of Jena and Auerstädt hid the danger and terrors of that ill-starred battle ! — Ah, my sons, you are at an age when your understanding can grasp these heavy afflictions. Call back to memory, in the future, when your mother and Queen is no longer living, this unhappy hour ; weep tears as you remember me, as I now at this sad moment lament the downfall of my fatherland. But let not tears alone content you ; act, develop your powers. Perhaps Prussia's tutelary genius will alight upon you ; then deliver your people from the disgrace, from the reproach, of degradation in which she languishes. Seek to win back from France the tarnished fame of your ancestors, as your grandfather, the Great Elector, avenged at Fehrbellin the defeat and disgrace of his father on the Swedes. Oh, my sons, do not allow yourselves to be swept along by the degeneracy of this age; become men, and covet the glory of great commanders and heroes. If you should lack in ambition, you would be unworthy of the name of princes and grandsons of the great Frederick. If with every exertion you cannot raise up again the prostrate state, then seek death as Louis Ferdinand sought it."

Although the men that surrounded the unfortunate King counseled surrender to the conqueror, at his discretion, one woman saw rescue only in a prolonged resistance. With a greatness of soul which, the Chamberlain von Schladen wrote in his diary, raised her "above every event," she expressed her views about those men who had contributed to her country's misfortunes. She fell into the greatest excitement when, without mercy, all the foul slanders that Napoleon had caused to be spread everywhere against her were communicated to her. At his command, these had been even publicly printed in Berlin. " With streaming eyes the noble Queen repeated the expressions of this scandalous libel. " No! " she cried. " Is it not enough for this wicked man to rob a King of his estates? Must also the honor of his wife be sacrificed, because he is base enough to publish about me the most shameful falsehoods ? "

Well might the Queen, in looking back upon

her own life, have felt personally lifted above that lying insult; yet in dark hours she kept before her the question whether the state and the people and her own family were not mistaken in resisting the visitations of fate. What Louise felt in such moments of anxious suspense, bowed under the weight of the power of fate, the words of Goethe express, which she wrote in her diary on the 5th of December, 1806. I mean the words from " Wilhelm Meister : " —

> " Wer nie sein Brod in Thränen ass,
> Wer nie die kummervollen Nächte
> Auf seinem Bette weinend sass,
> Der kennt euch nicht, ihr himmlischen Mächte !

> " Thr führt ins Leben uns hinein,
> Thr lasst den Armen schuldig werden ;
> Dann überlasst ihr ihn der Pein,
> Denn alle Schuld rächt sich auf Erden." [1]

At Königsberg the weak body of the heroic-souled woman succumbed to the blows of fate

[1] " Who never ate his bread in sorrow,
> Who never spent the darksome hours
> Weeping and watching for the morrow,
> He knows ye not, ye gloomy powers.

> " To earth, this weary earth, ye bring us,
> To guilt ye let us heedless go ;
> Then leave repentance fierce to wring us, —
> A moment's guilt, an age of woe."
>
> THOMAS CARLYLE.

coming upon her from all directions. Having fallen ill of a nervous fever, which had brought one of her children, Prince Carl, to the verge of the grave, she was in imminent danger for two weeks. Not quite recovered, she had to leave the old coronation city of the Prussian Kings, and to seek an asylum in the most remote corner of the monarchy, in Memel, because the divisions of the hostile army advanced farther and farther. "I prefer to fall into the hands of God rather than into the power of that man," she declared to Hufeland, the physician to the King. January 3d, in the severest cold, during a most fearful storm of driving snow, she was put into a carriage, and transported twenty miles over the Curish flat coasts to Memel. "We spent three days and nights on the journey, our road covered partly by the stormy waves of the ocean, partly by the ice ; the nights we passed in the most wretched quarters. The first night, without nourishing food, the Queen lay in a room whose windows were broken, and where the snow blew upon her bed." In Memel, where she joined her husband and children, her condition was improved, and the situation of military and political affairs justified new hopes. The remnant of the Prussian army, led by General Lestocq, combined at last with the advancing Russian troops, and in heroic contests not only restored Prussia's military honor, but seemed to hold out the possibility of obtaining by their valor, and with the aid of the allies, a passable peace.

In the battle at Eylau, where Lestocq accomplished marvels of bravery with six thousand men, Napoleon suffered such severe losses that, notwithstanding his official report of a victory, he offered to make a favorable peace with the King, if he would break off with his ally, the Emperor Alexander. This proposal Frederick William rejected decidedly. Louise hoped for further successes in the continued struggle when the Emperor Alexander came to Memel, and in the presence of his guards pledged his faith to the King. " This glorious union," she wrote to her father, "founded in misfortune, supported by steadfast faith, furnishes the strongest hope for endurance. I am convinced that sooner or later we shall conquer through constancy."

In April the Queen went to Königsberg, to visit her sister Frederika, living there, and passed some weeks in seeking to mitigate the miseries of war, and in helping to care for the wounded and destitute. But further advances of the French, the fall of the fortress of Danzig, and the menacing of Königsberg, caused her to return to Memel in the beginning of June. Here she faced the severest trials, when the battle of Friedland destroyed all hopes, when Königsberg fell, and the Russian forces withdrew, and Napoleon shifted his head-quarters to Tilsit.

She says, in a letter to her father, June 17th, " Again a terrible trouble has come upon us. We are on the point of forsaking the kingdom. Con-sider how I feel in so doing, but I implore you do not misjudge your daughter. Do not believe that pusillanimity bows my heart. There are two principal reasons why I am lifted above every-thing. The first is the thought, we are no sport of blind chance, but we are in God's hand, and his Providence guides us. The second is, we shall go down with honor. The King has demon-strated to the world that he does not wish dis-honor, but honor. Prussia would not voluntarily wear the chains of slavery. The King could not have acted differently without becoming untrue to his character and his people. Only he who has a true feeling of honor can know what support this thought gives." " I am going," she says, later, " as soon as the danger is imminent, to Riga. God will help me live through the moment when I must pass over the frontiers of this realm. There will be a need of strength, but I shall turn my eyes to Heaven, from whence come both good and ill, and it is my firm belief that He

will not send more than we are able to bear.
Once more, dear father, we shall go down with
honor, esteemed by nations, and shall ever have
friends, because we deserve them. I do not need
to tell you how consoling this thought is. I shall
endure all with such repose and calmness as peace
of conscience and pure trust can give. Therefore
be convinced, dear father, that we shall never be
wholly unhappy, and that many a one burdened
with a crown and prosperity is not so happy as
we. For your comfort, I will say that never has
anything been done on our side that is not con-
sistent and does not comport with the strictest
honor. Do not think of the details of our miseries. ˙ This I know will console you, as well as all
who belong to me. I am ever your faithful, obe-
dient daughter, who loves you warmly, and thanks
God that she can say so. — Your friend, Louise."
Some days later, after the conclusion of the arm-
istice between Napoleon and Alexander, she adds,
"To live and die in the way of right, and, if
need be, eat bread and salt, will never make me
wholly unhappy, but I can no longer hope. If
good fortune comes, oh, no one will receive it
more gratefully than I; but I no more expect it.
If misfortune comes, it will stun me for a time.
When not deserved it can never overwhelm me.
Only wrong on our part would bring me to the

grave. That will never take place, for we stand too high."

Thus, by a consciousness of honor and right, the spirit of the royal woman was cheered, when she was in danger of being driven over the borders of the lost kingdom into banishment. This cup was spared her, but what awaited her at the headquarters of the arrogant victor at Tilsit put her magnanimity and readiness to make sacrifices to a scarcely less severe test.

It is known that after the truce concluded reluctantly by Alexander, Napoleon cleverly succeeded in ensnaring him by his flattering arts, so that the easily moved Tsar entered into terms of peace and friendship with him, and laid Prussia's fate in the hands of an embittered and insolent foe. This he did notwithstanding his pledged word to his ally, notwithstanding the new assurance of fidelity given recently in the presence of the troops. We know, also, in what manner the French Emperor displayed to the utmost his conqueror's pride at Tilsit. Only out of regard for the Emperor who had recently become his ally would he allow the wrecks of the Prussian monarchy to exist.

Then it was that the noble Queen brought to the seriously imperiled state a sacrifice of self-renunciation which it would have been better not

to have demanded of her. After Alexander had
shown such a lamentable weakness in his relations with Napoleon, and, as one might say, had
betrayed the allies, recognizing the power that
the noble appearance of Louise, her character and
speech, exercised over the minds of men, he advised that she attempt to obtain by entreaty more
just conditions from the mercy of this powerful
man, who had so deeply injured the unhappy lady
by his base contumely and derision. Could one
have expected from the soldier Emperor, intrins-
ically brutal at heart, from this perfectly selfish
man, that he would bow before the greatness of
soul and the moral nobility of a conquered Queen?

Louise did not hesitate to do what was desired
of her, but she did it with a sorely wounded
heart. With indignation she had heard at Memel
that Napoleon manifested to her husband, who
had gone on before to Tilsit, studied indifference
and coldness. The unhappy husband, in his hon-
orable and open way, did not know how to flatter,
but with a feeling of his kingly worth he met the
haughty victor with noble pride. What he could
not obtain, should she seek to attain through her
woman's tact? We can comprehend that the letter that bade her come to Tilsit caused her many
tears. "Never shall I forget," writes her physician, Hufeland, "the moment when the noble

Queen received the King's command to come to
Tilsit, in order, if possible, to obtain still more
advantageous conditions of peace from Napoleon.
This she had not expected. She was beside herself. Amid a thousand tears, she said: 'This is
the most painful sacrifice that I can make for my
people, and only the hope of being useful to them
thereby can bring me to it.'" Louise says in her
diary: "God knows what a struggle it cost me!
For although I do not hate the man, yet I look
upon him as the one who has made the King and
his land wretched. I admire his talents. I do
not like his character, which is obviously treacherous and false. It will be hard for me to be
polite and courteous to him. But just this hard
thing is required of me. I am accustomed to
make sacrifices."

July 4th, the Queen drove to the village of
Picktupönen, situated in the neighborhood of Tilsit, whither the King, and on the following day
the Emperor Alexander, came. In regard to the
pending questions, Louise allowed herself to be
accurately instructed by Minister Hardenberg,
whose dismissal Napoleon had just succeeded in
obtaining. In answer to her greeting, the French
Emperor sent General Caulaincourt. At the same
time he inquired if Her Majesty would do him

the honor of dining with him. As soon as she arrived in the city he hoped to visit her.

Under the escort of French dragoons, on the afternoon of July 6th, Louise reached the dwelling of the King in Tilsit. A quarter of an hour later, Napoleon drove up to the door of the house. At the foot of the staircase he was received by the Oberhofmeisterin von Voss and the Countess Tauentzien. "He was," reported the first-mentioned lady, "very polite, talked a long time with the Queen, and drove away. Toward eight o'clock, we repaired to him, since out of regard for the Queen he had ordered an early dinner. During dinner he was in good humor, and talked much with the Queen. After dinner he had a long conversation with her. She was quite satisfied with the result. God grant that it may help to some purpose."

From another quarter we know that the Queen, after the dinner, returned to Picktupönen with the most sanguine hopes; yes, that even after the first conversation with Napoleon, full of joy, she believed that she had attained her purpose, and had induced her foe to more equitable conditions of peace.

Some of the words spoken at this memorable meeting have become known, especially the beautiful answer which Louise gave to the haughty

Emperor in response to the disdainful question, " But how could you ever begin war with me ? " " Sire," answered the Queen, " Even if we have been imposed upon in other respects, could the glory of Frederick deceive us in regard to our powers? " Quick-witted, full of spirit and fine tact, the Queen ever kept her ground as the mistress of the conversation. Her noble grace made such a deep impression on the hard soldier nature that the Emperor was, against his inclinations, exceedingly polite, and by no means repulsed her representations and petitions.

On the following day, when those about the King cherished the hope that Napoleon, moved by the humiliation of the unfortunate Queen, would really moderate his demands, Count Goltz, returning from an audience with the Emperor, announced that he had already revoked what he had promised the previous day, and had even gone still farther in the severity of his demands than before the interview with her. " All," he declared with bluntness, " all my words to the Queen were only polite phrases, that bind me to nothing ; for I am resolved to give the King the Elbe as a frontier line. There will be no negotiating farther, for I have already planned everything, in concert with the Emperor Alexander, whose friendship I prize. The King owes

his position only to the knightly adherence of this
monarch, since without this my brother Jerome
would have become King of Prussia, and the
present dynasty have been expelled." It was the
common report that Talleyrand was to blame for
Napoleon's not allowing himself to be softened.
"Sire, shall posterity say that on account of a
beautiful woman you have not duly profited by
your fairest campaign?" With such words the
diplomatist is said to have counseled his imperial
master to the severity which he stood in danger
of moderating.

Under such circumstances, when Louise and
her husband were once more invited by Napoleon
to dinner, she could only go with the deepest re-
luctance. "Napoleon," the Oberhofmeisterin reports, "looked embarrassed, and at the same time
treacherous and malicious. The company soon
took their seats at table. The conversation was
constrained and monosyllabic. After dinner the
Queen talked once more with Napoleon; on going
away, she told him that she was about to depart,
and felt deeply that she had been deceived." She
repeated the same when General Duroc, on the
next day, brought her the Emperor's parting com-
pliments: "She had not believed it possible that
she could be so duped."

In the last conversation Louise sought to wring

from the hard conqueror at least the promise that he would leave to the King strong Magdeburg on the left bank of the Elbe ; but the Emperor remained, as he says of himself in a letter to his wife, Josephine, " like a waxed cloth, from which all this slipped off." Louise, on the other hand, says, a year later, in calling to mind this talk with Napoleon : " Ah, what a recollection ! What I suffered then, I suffered more on account of others than on my own account. I wept ; I implored in the name of love and of humanity, in the name of our misfortunes and of the laws which govern the world. I was only a woman, a weak being, and yet raised above this adversary, so unfeeling and hard of heart." The story may be doubted that at her departure Napoleon offered her a fresh rose, which the Queen first declined, but, overcoming herself, then accepted, with the words, sounding like a condition, " At least with Magdeburg. " Napoleon answered harshly, " I must remark that it is I who give roses, and it is you who receive them." The fact is, however, true and well attested, that the unhappy Queen, on going away, complained to Napoleon unreservedly in regard to the deception prepared for her.

Even less pleasantly passed the conversation which, two days later, the afflicted but dignified

King held with the arrogant and powerful man.
The French did not refuse Frederick William
recognition, because he did not conceal his true
feelings and would in no wise humble himself
before the victor. Napoleon, also, did not conceal his feelings; with great harshness, he said
the most irritating and cutting things to the
King.

The Peace of Tilsit was humiliating and bitter
enough, without these undeserved mortifications.
While the King lost the half of his territory, the
other half was left to him, to be sure, but as a
" testimonial of the respect " which Napoleon
cherished for the Emperor Alexander. Russia
enlarged her borders with a piece of Prussia, by
way of return for the fidelity of an ally. The
agreement concerning the evacuation of Prussia
by the French troops concluded by Kalkreuth
July 12th, with criminal inattention, was utterly
ruinous. The treaty made the departure of the
hostile army dependent on payments, which the
victor had resolved to increase beyond what could
be supplied. Henceforth, mutilated, defenseless,
and exhausted, Prussia was given wholly into
Napoleon's hands. At pleasure, he could put an
end to the hated state, and more than once he
threatened to do so, in reality.

" My poor Queen is wholly in despair," wrote

the Countess Voss, after the last talk with Napoleon. Even more painfully in the coming days
the Queen felt that all she had done for the sake
of the King, her children, and the people, for the
mitigation of the fate of the state, had been in
vain. She appeared sad and cast down, and spent
many gloomy hours in tears. "The poor Queen
weeps too much." However, her strong soul did
not succumb to grief. She comforted herself with
a trust in God, and the consciousness that the
King had acted only in accordance with honor.
She believed all the more in the better future of
Prussia, since the entire range of the Peace of
Tilsit could not be seen.

"Peace is concluded," she wrote to Frau von
Berg, "but at a painful price: our frontier will
in the future extend only to the Elbe. Neverthe-
less the King is greater than his adversary. He
might have made an advantageous peace at Eylau: there he would have entered into negotiations voluntarily with an evil genius, with whom
he would have been obliged to ally himself. Now,
he has made a peace forced by necessity, and will
not league himself with him. This will one day
prove a blessing to Prussia! Also he must in
that case have deserted at Eylau a true ally; this
he would not do. It is my firm belief that this
course of action will bring good-fortune to Prussia."

Thus the noble-minded Queen was enabled to be a support to the King in the severe trials that befell him. It is not true that Frederick William, in stepping back into a place without rank, and in relinquishing the government to more fortunate hands, ever entertained the thought of yielding to destiny. It is also not correct that the King ever lacked in his outward appearance that firmness and dignity which became a Prussian monarch. He perhaps showed himself so depressed and sad, when engaged in familiar conversation, that, as the Countess Voss says, " it touched one's heart to the quick, and one could not listen to him without hot tears." Then the King needed all the consolation and strength which a close union with his noble wife could furnish him. " The Queen," the oft-quoted diary informs us, " now goes walking every morning and every evening alone with the King, and she is with him as much as possible, in order to cheer him." Supported by her love, Frederick William found strength to exercise the duties of a royal office under the most difficult circumstances conceivable, while he willingly resigned what usually makes the life of a prince attractive.

The royal household was reduced to what was most necessary. Servants and equipages were lessened ; costly liveries were given up; even the great service in gold plate, an heir-loom of their ancestors, was coined into money, to make payments for the land and the heavily oppressed subjects. To the same end, Louise gave away, when the need grew constantly greater, her brilliants, and retained only one ornament of pearls, which, according to her own expression, she loved more than her diamonds, and considered more suitable for her; "for pearls betoken tears, and I have shed so many of these."

The Queen indeed dispensed with external ornaments in these days of misfortune, and everything that surrounded her was plain and simple. The royal table in Memel was so frugally appointed that one could dine better at the family table of burghers. In the midst of these privations which the royal family, in noble resignation, imposed upon themselves did the Queen present a most sweet and exalted pattern. "Not a thousand court feasts, with golden uniforms and stars," said a Russian diplomatist, who spent a night at Memel with the royal family, "would I give in exchange for the memory of that night. A Queen sits at a poorly furnished table, that, like herself, is divested of all external adornments; but her grace, beauty, and dignity shine all the brighter. By her side sits the eldest Princess, Charlotte, as the bud by the unfolded rose. She shared with her mother the little household duties. Both delighted by their amiable attentions, and left behind in my soul a living picture, which no after-event can efface."

Previously, the Queen had kept herself aloof from public affairs, and avoided with just tact exercising influence, or even wishing to show outwardly anything different from perfect conformity with the will of the monarch. " She disdains," says Frau von Berg, in a letter addressed to Baron vom Stein, " the little expedients which power might afford her; one must esteem her the higher. Feeling her duty as a wife, she shares all the King's sympathies and opinions, defending those that he defends. Could one reproach her for that ? Meanwhile, the misfortunes have been so great and cruel that her eyes are opened to many things. She is a mother, and she cannot permit the future of her son, of her children, to be a matter of indifference; for this reason, she clings closely to her country."

The afflicted condition of the state, after the great catastrophe, naturally procured for her influence on many decisions of the King. It happened, with her coöperation, that Frederick William, soon after the conclusion of the unlucky peace, made up his mind to intrust the restoration of the fallen state first of all to the man whom posterity as well as his own age has honored as the restorer of Germany, the Baron vom und zum Stein. Sprung from an old knightly family on the Lahn, educated by worthy, strictly religious parents in the good old training, Stein, when a young man, had entered the state service of Frederick the Great. As Councilor of Mines, he was active in Westphalia. He rose step by step, thanks to his eminent talents and the excellency of his character, until he stood as President of the Westphalian Chambers, and at the head of the civil government there. In 1802 the proposal was made to him to enter the service of Hanover. This he declined, stating this memorable reason: that his conviction of the necessity of a union of the scattered and dismembered powers of Germany would not be compatible with the discharge of the duties which he should then have to assume. He saw the future of Germany in Prussia, and therefore devoted himself entirely to this state.

Soon Baron vom Stein was appointed by King Frederick William III., Minister of Commerce and Trade. As minister of a department, he could exercise no influence on the great policy, but only in his Bureau introduce many important improvements. He foresaw that the short-sighted and weakly guided state was steering towards a precipice. He represented in a memorial presented to the Queen the necessity of dismissing the Privy Council and Minister Haugwitz. He did not gain his object, but rather drew upon himself the censure of the King. Only too soon did the catastrophe which he had predicted, but could not avert, come. After the battle of Jena, when the other ministers lost their heads, he saved and carried to Königsberg the funds of his department, and thus furnished the means of at least restoring Prussia's military honor in the campaign of 1807. When, at last, Frederick William removed the corrupt Haugwitz forever from the helm of the state, he offered Stein the Bureau of Foreign Affairs. Stein proposed Hardenberg for this place, and considered himself better fitted for the Bureau of Finance, which, however, he would superintend only on condition that the King wholly break up the Cabinet, with its hindering influence. Thereupon arose a violent conflict in January, 1807, and Stein was dismissed in disgrace.

No one grieved more keenly for the loss of the great statesman than the Queen. "You were here," she wrote later to her confidential friend, Frau von Berg, "when Stein fell, — when his power, in such a wholly undeserved way, came to an end. You know, too, how it affected me:

how much anxiety I endured in regard to the re-
sults; how dissatisfied I was with everything."

Deeply wounded, Baron vom Stein retired to his
ancestral home in Nassau. But the calamities of
his Fatherland moved the great patriot more than
the injuries he had received. He was still ill
of a fever at home, when, after the Peace of
Tilsit, the King honorably recalled him as the
only man who could bring help. Stein did not
withhold his services. Still suffering in body, he
set out for distant Memel, upborne by the hope
that he should succeed in rebuilding the prostrate state, in filling the people with a new spirit,
and in rousing all their strength for the deliverance of the fallen Fatherland.

Queen Louise looked with eagerness for the
arrival of the great statesman. When, in the beginning of September, it was reported by Kno-
belsdorf, from Paris, that despotic France sought
to profit to the utmost by the right of the
stronger, Louise, almost in despair, broke forth
in the following words: "Ah, my God, why hast
thou forsaken me?" At the same time she cried
with ardent longing, "Why does Stein tarry?
He is my last hope. With his great heart and
comprehensive mind he will perhaps know of expedients which are hidden from us." "Stein is
coming," she says, in another letter, "and with

him I begin to see light." Later, she writes,
" How happy I am that Stein is again here ; yes,
I feel, since I know that he is at the head of
affairs, as if I could raise higher and carry more
easily my head, burdened with a weight of care."

The Queen was right in greeting Stein as a
helper in need. The day on which this statesman, received by the King with complete confidence, took the head of affairs, can be designated
even to-day as the beginning of the new birth of
Prussia and the preparation for the deliverance
of all Germany. Of course we do not mean to
say that none of the far-reaching reforms, which
made the ministry of Stein forever memorable, as
for example, the emancipation of the peasants,
the municipal regulations, and his pioneer work
for the Estates of the Empire, had been in some
degree prepared for, in a preceding age. The
catastrophe of Jena and Tilsit gave, perhaps, the
mighty impulse to the accomplishment of that
which without this would have been advanced
only slowly or would not have been even touched.
The point in question was not alone the political organization of the people, but also a radical
change in the organization of the army, which, as
is well known, was taken in hand under Stein's
active interest, but in pursuance of Sharnhorst's
enthusiastic ideas. It was especially here that

the King, with deep insight and untiring effort, trod the path of epoch-making reforms.

But what has Queen Louise in common with that which Sharnhorst, Stein, and their co-workers in these days of peril accomplished? Nothing more or less than this : it was she, who, for those men, smoothed the ways at court and helped to overcome the difficulties, obstacles, and prejudices with which they had to contend. "I implore you," wrote Louise to Stein, soon after his coming, "have patience during the first months; the King will certainly keep his word. Beyme (a councilor of great influence) will leave, but not till we are in Berlin. Be compliant until then. I pray God that the good may not come to naught on account of the patience and delay of three months. I implore you for the sake of myself, my children, my country, the King, have patience!"

Often the Queen had personal intercourse with the leading statesmen, Stein, Sharnhorst, Gneisenau, and others. But most closely was she connected by friendship with the Princess Louise Radziwill, an enthusiastic admirer of Stein, as well as with the cultured and patriotic Princess Marianne, wife of the noble Prince William (youngest brother of the King and father of the Queen-mother of Bavaria). In this circle, one might call it the central point of the patriotic Reform

party, the affairs of the Fatherland were zeal-
ously supported. Often enough the task devolved
upon the Queen of strengthening, in her delicate
and winning way, her royal husband in his sentiments friendly to reform, and hostile to the still
powerful party of the selfish, idle, and cowardly.
Quite often she influenced by soothing, conciliat-
ing, and mediating, when Stein, who in his outward appearance proclaimed the born ruler rather
than the servant, the only one whom Sharnhorst
compared with Blücher as being wholly without
the fear of man, in his fiery zeal offended personal
views, and little regarded the usages of the court.

Without being intrusted with questions of administration and legislation, Louise shared the
views that animated the statesman, and perfectly
comprehended the ultimate object which the bold
Baron steadfastly pursued after his entrance into
office. Stein, as he himself says, started out with
the great idea of putting into the nation a moral,
religious, and patriotic spirit, of infusing into it
new courage, self - confidence, and readiness for
any sacrifice, in order to obtain independence from
foreign rule, and national prosperity ; and of seizing the first favorable opportunity for beginning
the bloody conflict hazardous for both parties.
In all this he was sure of the assent and support
of the Queen.

Other anxieties, troubles of the most painful
kind, soon followed. In the previously mentioned
agreement of July 12th, the gradual evacuation
of the territory, restored to the King by the
French, was made dependent on the payment, or
placing in security, of the war-contributions, whose
amount had not yet been estimated. General
Daru, in Berlin, intrusted with the formulation
of the demands, was expressly directed to make
them as extravagant as possible. He discharged
his commission with masterly rapacity, while the
French armies, in an unheard-of manner, exacted
from the subjects their last piece of property.
The French commanders, with exceptional insolence, removed as spoil, to Paris, from royal
castles, works of art and treasures of all kinds.
Finally, in October, the demands were fixed at
154,000,000 francs. The five best fortresses of
the land, garrisoned at Prussia's expense, with
40,000 men of the enemy's troops, were demanded
as pledges. Even Stein was in the presence of
the unbounded claims of the conqueror, as the
Queen says, " for the first time, *wie zu Stein.*"
" This is our dreadful condition, everything here
lies prostrate. All strength will soon forsake me,
too. It is fearful, terribly hard, especially since
it is undeserved! My future is most gloomy! If
we can only keep Berlin ; but often the thought

falls like a weight on my foreboding heart that it, too, will be torn from us and made the capital of another kingdom. In that case I have only one wish, — to go far away, to live as a private person, and to forget — if possible ! Ah, God, to what has Prussia come ! Forsaken on account of weakness, — persecuted out of sheer insolence, — weakened by misfortune, — thus must we perish !" If there is still deliverance the Queen hopes it only from Stein. "God be praised, that Stein is here ! This is a proof that God has not yet wholly forsaken us." A couple of weeks later, October 29, 1807, when crushing tidings again came from Berlin by Napoleon's plenipotentiaries, it was a consolation to her to express her pain to the sympathizing statesman and to hear his wise counsel. She ends a letter to him thus : "To what a pass has it come ! our death-sentence is spoken !"

It was determined, with the support of Russia, to try and influence Napoleon. The Queen set aside all thoughts of self, and addressed a letter to him. Then Prince William, the King's brother, was sent to Paris with commissions which Stein drew up. But Napoleon's crafty policy prolonged the negotiations until the summer of 1808. Until this time not forty but almost two hundred thousand Frenchmen remained on Prussian territory and lived at its expense.

The Queen, who expected her confinement, and suffered not a little in Memel by reason of the cold, humid air, had hoped toward the end of the year to be able to return to Berlin. She must have rejoiced when, at last, Napoleon was persuaded to order the evacuation of East Prussia. " The Queen," he caused to be announced to her, " can now go to Königsberg ; there is therefore no necessity for her to go to Berlin." " He is a villain without a conscience, a despicable man," adds the Countess Voss.

. The court and its appurtenances moved, January 15 and 16, 1808, to Königsberg, but not without expressing deep gratitude for the numerous and touching proofs of love and attachment which had been given to the royal pair by the inhabitants of Memel during this troublous time. The great misery that the war and occupation by the enemy had produced here did not prevent a hearty and festive reception. The Queen received from the citizens the present of a *chaise longue* of green velvet. In taking the Estates of Prussia as godparents, the King showed anew that it was a necessity of his heart to knit ever closer the bond between his family and his people. This bond was strengthened in the days of universal calamity, when Frederick William and Louise set an example to the whole nation of steadfastness, submission, and greatness of soul, as well as in alleviating the distress of others, and freely choosing privation.

In the spring the royal family moved from the Castle to the Hippel garden (Die Hufen), near the Steindammer Gate, and lived here, practicing retrenchment, as in Memel. The Queen read much, and devoted herself by preference to the study of the history of her own country. " I am busy reading history, and live in the past, because the future is no longer for me." Could Louise, in this quiet country life, retire wholly within herself, and be unmoved by the outer world and its troubles? It even seemed so. " I have good books, a good conscience, a good piano-forte ; and thus one can live more quietly amid the storms of the world than those who stir them up."

But soon great events claimed the attention of the Queen. Napoleon, with unheard-of craft, had dethroned the Bourbons in Spain, in order to elevate his brother to the dignity of king. Louise felt keenly what this wanton sport in Madrid and Bayonne augured for other courts dependent on Napoleon's mercy. " What do you say to the news from Spain ? " she writes to her trusted friend, Frau von Berg. " Are they not new finger-traces of the iron hand which so heavily rests on the bowed brow of Europe ? A warning are

they not also for us? In the midst of peace, to
banish his first allies! To sow the seed of discord
between father and son! To tear the *infante*
from his father's heart, from his country! What
have we, we in our situation, to await?" —
That which followed the dethroning of the Bourbons in Spain would have a still· higher signifi-
cation for Prussia. That marvelous uprising of
the Spanish people against Napoleon's foreign
usurpation, could it not also in Prussia, in all
North Germany, kindle the thought of national
self-help? England, whose troops were already
fighting against the French in the Pyrenean pe-
ninsula, would not let Germany want pecuniary
assistance. Austria was quietly making preparations for war. Prussia, thanks to the activity of
the King and his incomparable co-workers, could
furnish a well-equipped army of 50,000 men, and
Napoleon, in order to quell the insurrection in
Spain, would have to withdraw the greatest part
of his troops in Germany. What if Prussia, then,
in unison with Austria, should begin the decisive
conflict, and take advantage of the animosity that
prevailed in all Northern Germany toward the
oppressor, for the deliverance of the Fatherland?
Was not this decided and bold policy to be pre-
ferred to the unworthy dependence which Napoleon sought to perpetuate? Just then, the nego-

tiations in Paris, in regard to the evacuation of Prussian territory, took the most critical turn. Entrance into the Confederation of the Rhine was demanded. Napoleon, before he set out for Spain, wanted to assure himself positively of the subordination of Prussia. At length, with this design in view, the treaty about which Prince William negotiated was to be concluded.

Like rocks on the sea-shore stood now in Königsberg the men of ardent sentiments and determined action, — such as Stein, Sharnhorst, and Gneisenau, — opposed to the partisans of a policy friendly to the French, to the unprincipled and cowardly. The King hesitated before taking the responsible resolution that might lead to Germany's deliverance and Prussia's destruction, and waited for the arrival of the Russian Emperor, since he considered success impossible without Russian consent. In the middle of September Alexander arrived at Königsberg, on his journey to Erfurt. In vain were all the efforts of Stein to lay before him the dangers of his policy so friendly to France. On the other hand, Alexander promised to do what he could for Prussia with Napoleon, at Erfurt, and the King and Queen now hoped everything from him.

In the mean time, there appeared in the newspapers a letter of Baron vom Stein, intercepted by the French authorities, wherein the secret thoughts of the bold statesman were imprudently disclosed. Stein's position was endangered. Seizing the opportunity, numerous and very powerful foes in Königsberg and Berlin worked both in public and in the dark for the fall of the Minister and his system. Even the King believed that he could no longer retain Stein without danger to the state. Or ought he, notwithstanding the dissuasions of Russia, to rush with Austria into the struggle against the tyrant of Europe? Then the King, without consulting Stein, ratified the disastrous Treaty of Paris, which imposed on the land exorbitant sacrifices, limited the army to 42,000 men, and bound Prussia by an oath to take the position of an auxiliary power, in the wars of France. Stein asked for his dismission and received it, but only after a delay of weeks, and with expressions of warm thanks for his unmeasured services. But Napoleon hurled from Spain, at the fallen statesman, that notorious decree which declared a "certain Stein," who sought to stir up sedition in Germany, an enemy of France and the Confederation of the Rhine, confiscated his estates and ordered his arrest, wherever he might be found. The outlaw fled to Austria; from thence he went later to Russia, and, at the side of the Emperor Alexander, did his best for the deliverance of Germany and Europe.

But what did Queen Louise in those critical days, when the point in question was the downfall of the Minister whom she so highly regarded, or the bold execution of his plans at home and abroad ?   " I suffer," she wrote to Frau von Berg on the 8th of July, 1808, " I suffer unspeakably. Only too often reproaches fall on me — on me who bear a burden of sorrows as Atlas bore the world.   What answer can I return ?   I sigh, and check my tears."

Who can doubt that Louise stood now, as before, on the side of the determined patriots.   If, however, she did not satisfy these, rather seemed to lend an ear to the adversaries of Stein, it happened only because she could not do otherwise. For if men on whom she could bestow confidence represented Stein to her as a desperate man, who would set himself, with the King, on a powder keg, in order to blow himself up, who can blame the Queen because she was filled with fear for her husband, her children, her people ?

Even in regard to another question in dispute, Stein and his friends did not see the Queen act in accordance with her own opinion.   The Emperor Alexander had invited the royal pair to visit him in St. Petersburg.   Stein advised them not to go. The Queen declared herself in favor of it, perhaps with the hope of binding Russia, the last prop of the imperiled state, more firmly to Prussia; perhaps, also, from fear of the return to Berlin demanded by the French, where, according to the judgment of Stein, who often enough had warned them of the fate of the Spanish Bourbons, the King would find himself in a mouse-trap, out of which the French would not again let him escape.

Towards the end of the year, the King and the Queen set out for St. Petersburg. The hearty reception, planned on a very grand scale, was followed by brilliant festivities. No less than 16,000 persons were invited to a masked ball, and at another time a ball-room was radiant with 20,000 tapers, besides 6,000 lamps.

Did Louise find pleasure in all this glitter? She felt her heart more oppressed than cheered, and even the studied attentions with which the imperial family, and especially Alexander, distinguished her, could not banish a certain melancholy. " I have returned as I went," she wrote to Frau von Berg, having arrived at Königsberg again after an absence of six weeks. " Nothing will blind me any more, and I say to you again : my kingdom is not of this world ! "

Different and yet somewhat similar may have been the impression which the King brought away from the Russian capital. The counsel of his imperial friend to reserve himself by a quiet

endurance of the present oppression, in lieu of
which Alexander promised to break forth, with
him, at a fitting time, had not failed of its effect.
The ministers entering upon office after Stein's
dismission counseled the King to take an active
part in the war soon to break out between Austria and France as the only way to save himself
and his people. Their advice was not taken.
The reorganization of the army, the providing of
war materials, the equipment of the fortresses,
had advanced so far by spring, that by taking advantage of the secret confederations spread over
North Germany, and by entering into a close
union with Austria, Prussia's prospects of success
seemed favorable. The King distrusted, we dare
not say without cause, the preparations for the
uprising of the people, as well as Austrian weap-
ons and Austrian policy. Meanwhile Prussia held.
herself in readiness for war, the payments to
France were discontinued, and it appeared to need
only an Austrian victory to bring things to a
crisis. Those were days of the greatest excitement; the uprising in the Tyrol, the calling to
arms in Hesse by Dörnberg, Schill's marching
out of Berlin with his hussars, kept all souls
breathless. Of course, the King had to censure
and punish Schill's attempt; but when the fearful battle at Aspern checked Napoleon's victo-

rious march, the time seemed to have come for
Prussia to act. But the King delayed his decision. "There is yet time," he said, in reply to
the Austrian negotiator; "give the enemy another blow, and we are united." But the blow at
Wagram failed of the intended effect; the truce
of Znaim was concluded, the Tyrolese heroes still
fought in an unequal contest, and at last came
peace, and Austria's alliance with Napoleon.

We cannot doubt that Louise followed with
anxious attention the events in the Austrian field
of war, the rash deed of Schill, and the sad fate of
his band of heroes, and that she sincerely wished
for Prussia's entrance into action; but we do not
know whether, after the treaty concluded with
Napoleon, after such relations with Russia, and
after considering the entire situation of the State,
she could advocate war. The Queen has only told
us what she suffered, not what she did. She
wrote on the 12th of March, 1809, two days after
her thirty-second birthday, "I have to-day suffered as if the world with all its sins were rest-
ing upon me. I am ill, and I think that so long
as affairs go on thus I shall never recover." She
then expressed her fear that Russia, in the im-
pending war, would be forced at last, by its new
connection with Napoleon, to fight with France
against Austria. The sequel might be that Prus-

sia, too, must go over to that side. " Prussia
against Austria! What is to become of Germany? No, I cannot express what I feel; my
heart feels as if it would burst! And we are here
in this banishment, in this climate, where all
storms rage, remote from everything homelike.
O God, have we not yet had trials enough?"
"My birthday," she continues, "was to me a
dreadful day. In the evening, a great, splendid
feast, which the city gave in my honor; previous
to that a rich, gay banquet at the Castle, — it is
not possible to tell you how sad all has made me!
My heart was rent; I danced, I smiled, I said
pleasant things to the givers of the feast; I was
friendly towards every one, and in my distress I
did not know which way to turn! To whom a
year hence will Prussia belong? Whither shall
we all be scattered? Almighty Father, have Thou
compassion!"

That which Louise had most dreaded, the union
of Prussian troops with French, did not take place,
but the war brought her sorrow and anxiety
enough. "Ah, God, much has befallen me. Thou
alone canst help, — I look for no future on earth.
God knows where I shall be buried: scarcely on
Prussian soil. Austria will sing her swan song,
and then farewell Germania!"

About the same time, in the summer of the

year 1809, she addressed a letter to her beloved father, which so well discloses the greatness of her soul, the inner worth of her heart, that it deserves a place here.

In the first half of this long letter she lays before him her thoughts about the present condition of the world, and the future. She did not hope to obtain a better state of things for herself, but for the succeeding generation. Without misconstruing the historical warrant for the French Revolution, and for Napoleon's policy, she foresaw the future downfall of the new order of things, which the tyrant of Europe fancied he had founded so securely. She is firm in the belief of a moral order in the world, and in the final triumph of good.

" With us it is all over for the present, even if not forever. I look for nothing more during my life. I have resigned myself ; and in this resignation, in this submission to the will of God, I am now tranquil and at peace; if I do not possess earthly happiness I have what means more, — spiritual blessedness. It becomes more and more clear to me that everything had to come as it has. Divine Providence is unmistakably introducing a new order of things in the world ; there will be a different arrangement, since the old order has outlived itself and is falling to pieces. *We have*

fallen asleep on the laurels of Frederick the Great,
who, as the master of his century, created a new
epoch. We have not kept pace with the age,
therefore it has left us behind. No one is better
aware of this than the King. I have just had a
conversation with him, in which he repeatedly
said, as if speaking to himself: 'This also must be
changed among us.' Even the best and most ma-
turely considered plans fail, and the French Emperor is at least more cunning and astute. If the
Russians and Prussians had fought bravely as
lions, even if unconquered, we should neverthe-
less have been obliged to quit the field, the enemy would have had the advantage. We may
learn much from him, and what he has done and
achieved will not be lost upon us. It would be
blasphemy to say that God is with him; but evi-
dently he is an instrument in the hand of the Al-
mightly to bury the old era, which no longer has
life, but which is almost overgrown with excres-
cences.

"Better times will certainly come. Faith in the
most perfect Being is a guaranty for this. But
only through goodness can the world become better. Therefore, I do not believe that the Emperor Napoleon Bonaparte is firm and safe on his
glittering throne. Only truth and justice are
strong and secure. He is only politic, that means

worldly-wise, and he does not conform to eternal laws but to circumstances, as they happen to be. With such a policy he stains his government by many deeds of injustice. His intentions are not good, even if his cause is good. In his boundless ambition, he thinks only of himself and his personal interest. We must admire him, but not love him. He is dazzled by his success, and he fancies himself able to accomplish everything. Moreover, he has no moderation ; and he who cannot observe moderation loses his balance and falls. I have a strong faith in God, and also in His moral government of the world. This I do not see in the rule of might ; therefore, I have the hope this present evil age will be succeeded by a better one. All good men hope and wish for this, and await it, and one must not be misled by the panegyrists of present heroes, that seem to them great. What has taken place is unmistakably neither final nor abiding, nor for the best good of all, but only the opening of a path to a better end. This end appears to be at a great distance ; we probably shall not see it, and shall die before it is reached. As God wills ; all as He wills. But I find comfort, strength, courage, and serenity in this hope, which lies deep in my soul. Life is but a passage, yet we must go through it. Let us only care for this, to become each day riper and better.

"Here, dear father, you have my political creed, as well as a woman can construct one. It may have gaps, but I shall not suffer by that. But pardon me for annoying you with this; from it you can at least see that you have a pious and attached daughter, and that the principles of Christian piety, which I owe to your teachings and your godly example, have borne their fruits, and will bear them as long as I live."

The second half of this beautiful letter discloses to us a heart-stirring view of the conjugal and domestic life of the Queen.

"Gladly will you hear, dear father, that the calamities which have befallen us have not forced their way into our wedded and home life, rather have strengthened the same, and made it even more precious to us. The King, the best of beings, is kinder and more loving than ever. Often I think I see in him the lover and the bridegroom. Always showing more by his actions than by his words, I see the watchfulness that he has for me in all points. Only yesterday he said to me in his plain and simple way, looking at me with his true eyes: 'Thou, dear Louise! Thou hast become to me in misfortune still more precious and beloved. Now I know from experience what I have in thee. It may storm without, if only it remains fair weather in our wedded life. Because

I love thee so I have called our latest-born little daughter Louise. May she become a Louise.' — This goodness moved me to tears. It is my pride, my joy, and my happiness to possess the love and approval of this best of men; and because I heartily love him in return, and we are so united that the will of the one is also the will of the other, it becomes easy for me to preserve this happy union of sentiments, which has become closer with years. In a word, he pleases me in all points, and I please him, and we are happiest when we are together. Pardon me, dear father, that I tell this with a certain boastfulness. There lies in it the artless expression of my happiness, which interests no one in this world more deeply than you, dear, fond father! How to treat others; *that, too, I have learned from the King.* I cannot talk upon this subject it is enough that we understand it.

"Our children are our treasures, and our eyes rest upon them with satisfaction and hope. The Crown Prince is full of life and spirit. He has superior talents, which are happily developed and cultivated. He is true in all his sentiments and words, and his vivacity makes dissimulation impossible. He learns history with especial success, and the great and the good attract to them his imaginative mind. He has a keen appreciation of

what is humorous, and his comical and startling
ideas entertain us agreeably. He is especially attached to his mother, and he cannot be purer than
he is. He is very dear to me, and I often talk
with him of how it will be when he at some future day is King." — He who is acquainted with
the life of the talented, cultivated, and eloquent
Frederick William IV., will find the description
which his mother has given quite striking. This
King certainly was not lacking in mind, wit, or
heart, and how much he was alive to the political
thoughts which Louise stirred up in him he has
himself declared in the words : " *The unity of
Germany concerns me deeply : it is an inheritance
from my mother.*" However, the richly gifted
but gentle nature of Frederick William IV., was
not called to establish the unity and greatness of
Germany. This required, apart from the consum-
mation of the times, and the assistance of the
right men, an unusually manly and resolute en-
ergy, such as is inherent in the second son of
Louise. Of him she says, in the letter previously
quoted : —

"Our son William will be, if everything does
not deceive me, like his father : simple, upright,
and wise. Also, in his outward appearance he
bears the greatest resemblance to him, only he is,
I think, not so good looking. You see, dear father, I am still in love with my husband."

Prince William was then eleven years of age. The eye of the mother had correctly discerned the characteristics of his nature, but she could not know what rare and noble powers besides, still dormant in him, would wake to activity through time and its great events. " Our daughter Charlotte (later Empress of Russia) gives me more and more pleasure; she is, to be sure, reserved and introspective, but, like her father, hides behind an apparently cold exterior a warm, sympathizing heart. Seemingly indifferent, she has much love and interest. From thence it comes that she has a certain stateliness of manner. If God spares her life I anticipate for her a brilliant future. Carl is good-natured, mirthful, open-hearted, and gifted. He is developing in body as finely as in mind. He often has naïve ideas, which provoke us to laughter. He is bright and witty. His never-ending questions often embarrass me, because I cannot or I must not answer them, but this shows a desire for knowledge, and — sometimes, when he smiles slyly, also curiosity. He will pass through life lightly and joyfully, without losing interest in the weal and woe of others. Our daughter Alexandrina is, like other girls of her age and natural disposition, clinging and child-like. She shows a faculty of correct apprehension, a vivid fancy, and can often laugh heart-

ily. For what is comical she has sense and sus-
ceptibility. She has a turn for satire and looks
in saying satirical things very serious; this, however, does not harm her good-nature. Nothing as
yet can be said about little Louise. She has the
profile of her excellent father and the eyes of the
King, only somewhat lighter in color. Her name
is Louise; may she resemble her ancestress, the
amiable and devout Louise of Orleans, the esti-
mable wife of the Great Elector." — Louise became, as is known, the wife of Frederick, Prince
of the Netherlands ; Alexandrina, Grand Duchess
of Mecklenburg-Schwerin. The seventh of the
children, who survived their mother, was born
October 11, 1809, and therefore could not here
be mentioned.

This remarkable letter ends thus: "Here I
have presented to you, beloved father, my entire
gallery. You will say, this is a woman who dotes
upon her children, who only sees good in them
and has no eyes for their deficiencies and faults.
And truly I do not find in any a bad disposition that might make me anxious about the future. They have, like other human children, their
naughty ways, but these will disappear in time as
they become wiser. Circumstances and relations
train men, and it may be well for our children
that already in their youth they have learned to

know the serious side of life. If they had grown up in the lap of plenty and ease then they would suppose everything must ever be thus. But they see by the grave countenance of their father, and the grief and frequent tears of their mother, that things can change. It is especially salutary for the Crown Prince that he become acquainted with misfortune while Crown Prince. He will prize prosperity the higher and guard it the more carefully, when, as I hope, a better time will come for him. My solicitude is ever for my children, and I ask God daily in my prayers for them that He will bless them, and not take from them his good Spirit. I sympathize with my excellent physician, Hufeland, in this. He does not merely care for the physical well-being of my children, he is also mindful of their spiritual good; and the upright and ingenuous Borowsky, whose society the King enjoys and whom he loves, helps to the same end. May God preserve them to us, preserve my best treasures, whom no one can snatch from me. Come what will we shall be happy in one another and in our good children."

"I have written this to you, beloved father, that you may think of us without anxiety. I commend to your kind remembrances my husband, also all our children. who kiss the hands of their venerable grandfather. I am and remain, dear father, your grateful daughter."

A place may here be found for another word of
the noble Queen about her children. It includes
both a wish and a prophecy. "Even if posterity
does not mention my name among illustrious
women, yet, when it learns the sorrows of the
time, it will know what I have suffered through
them, and will say: She endured much, she remained patient in the midst of suffering. Then
I could wish that at the same time they might
say: She gave birth to children, who were worthy
of better times, she endeavored to lead them on
and at last her care has borne rich fruit."

In the summer of 1809 the Queen, who had
suffered so much in mind, began to suffer also in
body. An intermittent fever wasted her strength,
and earlier than usual she had to exchange her
country residence for the castle. The court
preacher, Borowsky, who had almost daily intercourse with her, and whose uprightness and sincerity Louise commended, stated at that time:
"Our dear Queen is, at this Lenten season, far
from joyful, but her seriousness has a quiet serenity, and the calmness and repose which God
gives her, sheds over her entire life a noble grace.
Her eyes, it is true, have lost their former sparkle,
and one sees that they have wept much, and still
weep; but by this they have received an expression of gentle sorrow and quiet longing, which is

even more charming than that which mere enjoy-
ment of life would give. The bloom on her countenance is indeed gone and a soft pallor over-
spreads it, yet her face is still beautiful, and now
the white roses on her cheeks please me almost
more than the red of other days. At times is
seen a slight trembling of the mouth, around
which formerly a sweet, happy smile hovered.
Sorrow is implied by this, but it is not bitter.
Her dress is ever exceedingly simple, and the
choice of colors indicates her frame of mind. The
piety of our honored Queen is sound, simple, natural, and perfectly in accordance with her sensi-
tive mind and disposition, far from everything
forced, artificial, and sentimental."

Louise was a genuine Christian, who with com-
posure and humility received all her sufferings as
dispensations sent from God for her purification.
Therefore the numerous disappointments and
mortifications did not steel her heart, rather this
remained open to kindness and love. To help her
fellow-men, to become useful to them, was and
remained to her a source of the purest joy.

With increasing interest the Queen devoted
herself to the advancement of the education of the
young. When she saw in St. Petersburg the noble institutions, founded by the Empress mother,
for the education of girls, she lamented that she

was not in circumstances to follow her example.
The Louise Institution in Berlin was founded one
year after the death of the Queen and dedicated
to her memory. The Orphanage in Königsberg
was, through her influence, managed after the
methods of Pestalozzi, and became a model train-
ing-school. The writings of the great teacher had
deeply interested her ; she invited a scholar of the
master, Director Zeller, to Königsberg, and sus-
tained him in his philanthropic exertions. She
did not disdain to visit the schools, and in an in-
telligent and enthusiastic manner acquiesced in all
that concerned teacher and pupil. When in Memel the subject of founding a university in Berlin
was agitated, Frederick William gave his assent
with the warm words: "That is right, that is
excellent; the State must recover through intellectual strength what it has lost through physical
force." In this Louise agreed entirely with her
husband.

The moral and religious elevation of the people
interested her deeply. Therefore she perceived
with joy the beginnings of a revival of religious
life, the precursors of that genuine, I might say,
noble piety, through which the people in the days
of calamity regained their moral strength. "Because we have back-slidden, therefore have our
misfortunes come," she declared, and to speak in

the words of a Russian historian, "in her living faith she was the silent guardian of every noble germ of the awakening Christian life."

But above everything else, she desired to rouse a national spirit. The setting up of monumental tablets in the churches, to the memory of warriors who had rendered service to their country, she hails as one of the sparks, "from which, perhaps, the flame of God can rise, which will consume the scourges of the people." She alludes to the Tyrol as well as to Spain, and extols Andreas Hofer, the brave leader of the Tyrolese. She longs to have a Maid of Orleans appear to vanquish the foe, the wicked foe. "Also in my Schiller," she continues, "I have read again and again. Why was he not induced to come to Berlin? Why did he die? I wonder whether the poet of Tell was also blinded as Johannes von Müller, the historian of the Swiss Confederacy! No! no! only read the passage. 'Base is the nation that does not risk all for its honor.' Can these words be false? And still I must ask: why did he die? Whom God in these times loves, He takes to himself!"

Long had the Queen desired to be able to take residence again in the capital of the land, which since the misfortune of Jena she had not visited. In a letter to her sister, Frederika, written in August, 1809, she says: "If only I could go to Berlin, thither, thither, I would like to go now, it is real homesickness which makes me long for it and my Charlottenburg." At last, on the 15th of December, the day of departure could be appointed. Then with the joy, gloomy forebodings were roused in her soul. "So I shall soon be in Berlin again, and restored to so many faithful hearts that love and esteem me. At the thought I am quite oppressed with joy. I shed many tears here when I think that I shall find everything so wholly different there. Dark forebodings distress me; I would like to sit alone and abandon myself to my thoughts. I hope it will be a change for the better."

Amid the most touching proofs of attachment and respect, which met the King and Queen from all directions, they moved as in a triumph from Königsberg to Berlin. The day of the festive entrance was December 23d. Louise was in a magnificent carriage, a gift from the citizens of Berlin, the King on horseback, the Crown Prince and Prince William on foot as officers of guards with her regiment.

As on this day, so as often as the Queen appeared in public, enthusiastic demonstrations of respect were paid her. When March 10, 1810, drew near the genial poet, Kleist, composed in

honor of the birthday of the Queen, a festive
poem, in which his respect, bordering on adora-
tion, has found a classical expression. Only the
beginning of the poem, to which later Kleist gave
the form of a sonnet, can here find a place.

> " Du, die das Unglück mit der Grazie Schritten
> Auf jungen Schultern herrlich jüngsthin trug,
> Wie wunderbar ist meine Brust verwirrt
> In diesem Augenblick, da ich auf Knien,
> Um Dich, zu segnen, vor Dir niedersinke,
> Ich soll Dir ungetrübte Tag' erfleh'n,
> *Dir, die der hohen Himmelssonne gleich,*
> *In voller Pracht erst strahlt und Herrlickkeit,*
> *Wenn sie durch finst're Wetterwolken bricht.*
> O, Du, die aus dem Kampf empörter Zeit,
> *Die einz' ge Siegerin hervorgegangen :*
> Was für ein Wort, Dein würdig, sag' ich Dir ? "

Louise's frame of mind was not in harmony
with the festive joy and splendor with which her
birthday was celebrated. She was full of anxious
solicitude for the State, whose imperiled condition, since the termination of the Austrian-French
war, had grown continually worse. Napoleon's
resentment was excited by the wavering attitude
of the Prussian government during the year 1809.
From the moment Napoleon alienated himself
from Russia, and formed a family alliance with
Austria, he had no longer any reason to show
regard for Prussia. He made his contempt and

hatred undisguised and evident, and only seemed to desire to drain the State before he annihilated it. Already the surrender of Silesia was hinted at as indemnification for the money due; again and again the fate of the Spanish Bourbons presented itself threateningly to the mind of the Queen. Had not Napoleon demanded the return to Berlin, in order to have the court wholly in his power? Could he not do with it what he liked? We know how much in earnest the Queen was, when on the fête-day, March 10th, she expressed her feeling to some confidential friends in the words: "I think this will be, perhaps, the last time that I shall celebrate my birthday here."

The Queen was induced to address once more a letter to Napoleon, which her sister, the Princess of Thurn and Taxis, delivered in Paris, March 15th. But the Emperor continued his insulting reproaches, threats, and demands; and even Altenstein, Minister of Finance, did not hesitate to advise the King to abandon Silesia to the oppressor. In furthering the appointment of the former Cabinet Minister, Hardenberg, to the head of the government, Louise rendered the land her last great service.

In the spring of 1810 the Queen was for a long time seriously ill. Lung difficulties, accompanied with fever, grew worse, until she had spasms.

The physicians in attendance cautioned against all excitement, at a time, when the heart of the Princess was more than ever solicitous for her husband, her children, and her people. However, she recovered, so far, in Potsdam, whither she moved at the end of April, that a long-cherished wish, to visit her father in Strelitz, could be realized.

Louise left Charlottenburg on the 24th of June. During the morning, as the Oberhofmeisterin, who accompanied her, tells us, the Queen was very cheerful. "But when we approached the frontier (Prussia-Mecklenburg), suddenly a mysterious melancholy came over her, but she quickly composed herself, and it passed off." Was it a dim foreboding of that which she was going to meet ?

In Fürstenberg, she was warmly welcomed by her father, and brothers, and sisters, in New-Strelitz, by her venerable grandmother. She felt herself even more blessed, when her husband reached her, June 28th. "I am very happy to-day, dear father, as your daughter, and the wife of the best of men," such were the last words that she wrote.

At the Villa of Hohen-Zieritz, whither the Duke went with his guests on the evening of this day, the Queen was taken ill. She had again trouble with her lungs, and a violent attack of fever. The Duke's physician, summoned hither, apprehended as yet no danger, and the King, called back by urgent business of State, left his sick wife, July 3d, with the hope of soon being able to return for her. Instead of this, he was himself taken ill in Charlottenburg, and only saw the Queen again when she was already struggling with death.

For ten days her condition continued almost unaltered; fever, a cough, and weakness, only the weakness grew greater and the breath shorter. But it is hardly necessary to say that the Queen bore her sufferings with patience and submission to God. Her thoughts lingered much with her husband and children. A letter from the King so rejoiced her, that she could not be separated from it. " Ah, what a letter," she said, more than once. " How happy is she who receives such letters ! "

Early in the morning of the 16th of July violent spasms in the chest set in, and the physicians, summoned hither from Berlin, considered the sick lady in great danger. The difficulty in breathing and the fever increased. In the night of July 18th the Queen, with uplifted hand, suddenly said to Heim, the physician, watching by her side: " Consider if I should be taken away from the King — from my children." Towards five o'clock, in the

morning of July 19th, the monarch, who had been
sent for by special messengers, arrived at Hohen-
Zieritz. "But the Queen," says the Countess
Voss, "had already death written on her brow.
And yet how did she receive her husband? With
what joy did she embrace and kiss him, while he
wept bitterly. The Crown Prince and Prince
William had come with him. As far as the poor
Queen was able, she tried still to speak. She
would so gladly have gone on talking with the
King, but could not; so it went on, and she grew
weaker and weaker. The King sat on the edge
of the bed and I knelt beside it. He endeavored
to warm the cold hands of the Queen; then he
held one hand and laid the other in my hands, in
order that I should rub it warm. It was about
nine o'clock. The Queen had turned her head
gently on one side, and raising her great, wide-
opened eyes steadfastly up to heaven, said: ' I am
dying. O Jesus, make it easy!' Sobbing, the
King fell back and hardly could he find self-com-
mand to close the eyes of the glorified one, those
eyes " which had so faithfully lighted up his dark
path.' "

Never did a people mourn more deeply for a
sovereign than did Prussia and a great part of
the rest of Germany for Queen Louise. The
grief was soon converted into a feeling of anger

and revenge, of revenge toward those who had tortured to death this noble woman. It was universally said that the foe had killed the tutelary goddess of the people ; and thus the name of the gentle, saintly sufferer became the watchword in conflict and war. "Our saint is in heaven," said Blücher, whom Louise esteemed highly, even as he reverenced his patriotic queen; and the hero felt more and more forcibly that he was chosen by Providence to become her avenger on the enemies of Germany. When, March 30, 1814, after all the bloody contests on German and French soil, he led his victorious army to the heights of Montmartre, and saw beneath his feet the great capital of France conquered, he gave expression to his thought in the proud words, "*Louise is avenged.*"

Not only brave warriors, but also patriotic poets of those days have exalted the name of Louise to a battle-cry. This clearly shows the feeling which ruled all hearts ; that at sight of the glorious marble figure of the sleeping Queen, which the master-hand of Rausch created for the beautiful mausoleum erected by Frederick William III. at Charlottenburg, not so much a thought of peace as of conflict moved the youthful Theodore Körner, when he sang : —

" Du schläfst so sanft, die stillen Züge hauchen
Noch Deines Lebens schöne Träume wieder;
Der Schlummer nur senkt seine Flügel nieder,
Und heiliger Frieden schliest die klaren Augen!

" So schlummere fort, bis Deines Volkes Brüder,
Wenn Flammenzeichen von den Bergen rauchen,
Mit Gott versöhnt die rostigen Schwerter brauchen,
Das Leben opfernd für die höchsten Güter!

" Tief führt der Herr durch Nacht uns zum Verderben,
So sollen wir im Kampf uns Heil erwerben,
Dass unsere Enkel freie Männer sterben!

" Kommt dann der Tag der Freiheit und der Rache,
Dann ruft dein Volk, dann, deutsche Frau, erwache,
Ein guter Engel für die gute Sache!" [1]

---

[1] " Thou sleep'st so soft! thy features in their sleep
Have all the beauty aye that life could bring;
Except that slumber waves o'er thee its wing,
And peace hath closed thine eyes, no more to weep!

" So slumber on, until thy people rise,
Waked by the flames on every beacon height,
And, wielding all their sabres for the fight,
Yield up their life a willing sacrifice!

" For Heaven now leads us through death and night,
And we must earn e'en with our warm life blood
The meed of freedom, life's divinest good.
Oh let it soon but dawn upon our sight!

" Then rouse thy nation; then, sweet saint awake,
A guardian angel, for thy people's sake!"

G. F. RICHARDSON.

When, three years after her death, the hour of
deliverance for the people struck and the glorious
struggles for independence began, the departed
one was the Lady of the Knighthood in the Wars
of Liberation. She inflamed, as Fouqué says,
from higher spheres the warriors of her royal
husband with a twofold enthusiasm for victory
or death.

Then sang with fervor and fire the poet of the
" Lyre and Sword " : —

> " So soll Dein Bild auf unsern Fahnen schweben,
>   Und soll uns leuchten durch die Nacht zum Sieg.
>   *Luise* sei der Schutzgeist deutscher Sache,
>   *Luise* sei das Losungswort zur Rache."

Not with such feelings did King William, July
19, 1870, on the sixtieth anniversary of the death
of Louise, make his annual visit to the mausoleum at Charlottenburg, to the tomb of his never-
to-be-forgotten mother. On this same day the
French declaration of war was delivered in Berlin. If the King, in memory of the sacred hour
when sixty years before he knelt by the death-
bed of his mother, gathered strength for the conduct of a difficult war, the issue was not a war of
revenge, but the warding off of a wanton attack
that the nephew and heir of the first Napoleon
had attempted against Germany. Perhaps no
thought came before the mind of the monarch

more clearly than this : that it would be important, after a victorious repulse of an arrogant enemy, to secure peace to Germany for the future in the way that Queen Louise had discerned as the only means of deliverance : namely, the closest union of all those who glory in their German name. The founding of the new Empire took place in the spirit of Louise ; its establishment was the fulfillment of her hopes and desires. Moral power is a nation's only strength. We trust, relying upon God, that the same spirit may even to the distant future rule the German Fatherland.